STEP

INTO

MY

FLOW

STEP INTO MY FLOW

A BOOK OF POETRY

MICHELLE HEIGHWAY

Special thanks to Toria Garbutt and the Arts Council England DYCP
Fund for making this book possible.

i4visuals / UK All rights reserved. This publication may not be reproduced, stored in a retrieval system or transmitted, in any form or by any means, electronic, mechanical, photocopying, recording or otherwise, without the prior permission of the publishers.

Layout: Zoe Norvell
Mentor: Toria Garbutt
Cover Design: Lynn Hatzius
Proofreading: Zoë Howe
Author Photograph: Matt Littlewood
Publisher: i4visuals

© 2025 Michelle Heighway
First published in Great Britain, 2025
ISBN 978-1-3999-9542-9

CONTENTS

SECTION 1:
Beginnings and Reflections 1

SECTION 2:
Nature and Healing 33

SECTION 3:
Loss and Longing 57

SECTION 4:
Celebration, Connection and Transformation 93

AFTERWORD
. . . . 117

GLOSSARY
. . . . 119

ABOUT THE AUTHOR
. . . . 120

SECTION 1

—

BEGINNINGS AND REFLECTIONS

TULIPS ON WEDNESDAY

Lungs open
In the morning light
Soothing the mind
Moments in time

Tulips on Wednesday
Deep pink
Smile at me through
Sun reflected windows

I am grateful
For another day
Another way to stay whole
To stay home
And nurture my
Divine feminine energy

I climb into the day
With a sense of belonging
I see you, universe,
And you see me

SPRING

Come on spring
I can smell you
In the air

Dry crisp morning
Still icy like December
But I love you

Come on crow
Tell me where you go?

On this spring feeling morning
No clouds in the sky
Higher vibrations
Clean air

I breathe you in

INCUBATE

The seed
Of the idea
Of you
It keeps me moving
Keeps me growing

Pure light
Delight
Delightful noise
Ambient sounds

In the seed
Of the idea
Of you
I feel calm

Patiently waiting
Creating
Creations I made
For you

In the seed
Of these ideas
I live

NEW ATMOSPHERE

I wanna be free
Free from
The many cages
I put myself into

My ribs hold me tight
I hide behind them
Cocoon inside them
With my heartbeat

Yet my spirit
Often dances
And tries to float
For a while
Like a perfume
Or a smoke trail

I hope to enter
New territories
A new atmosphere

I see freedom
To be me
To be free

TO THE SHORES

Would you follow me
To the shores
Of this life
I promise
I'll be kind

I'll give you
A surfboard to ride
The rough
And the smooth
Tides

We will be alright
You and me
I can feel it
I can see it

BUTTERFLY EFFECT

While most
Of them dream
She does

As she does
They see

As they see
She shines

As she shines
They know

As she flies
She finds

As she looks
She sees

She transcends

As she transcends
She transforms

Look a little deeper
It creeps on in
And YOU are gone

MAPLE SYRUP SKIES

Maple syrup skies
Dragonflies
Ice cream highs
And then there's you

Torrential rain
Heals the pain
Of saints and sinners
All the same

But sometimes
When a pin drops
The heavens
Spring open for you

Find a penny
Don't pick it up
Today you realise
You make your own luck

Tucked up in journals
Manifested dreams
Beams of light
Find you
Guide you

And the rabbit runs
And disappears
With the rain

I am sunshine
I am rainbows
I am light

I see me
I see you

NEW ORDER

And as the world finds another day
Bleeds light upon the shoulders
Of kings and queens
And all creatures
Great and small

Pollution rises
Population falls

The humdrum of vehicles
And the call of songbirds
Through stained windows
Continue

FAITH OR FAITHLESS

Cruising through time
The jackdaw cries
Afraid of the void

Classic example
Of the lack of faith
Nothing is nothing
Blank canvas
Black hole

Galaxies
Upon galaxies
Silent in space
Void

Keep cruising
Keep moving
Don't listen
To the cry

AND IN THE SHELL OF AN IDEA

And in the shell
Of an idea
I found Monday
Blue like sky
Fresh like green grass

In the eyes of Monday
I found something whole

Half forgotten
In lost nights
Of sleepless dreams
Fragmented now complete
I welcome Monday

I write you into my home
Warm like fresh baked bread
Fire flames through glass
On winter days

I found Monday
Monday found me

CELLS

Listen to every cell
In your body

Talk to them
The body
She hears you
Feels you

The mind is in control
Listen and speak kindly
As you run into today

IMAGINATION

Harnessing the power
Of imagination

Brings joy
That is unexplainable
Yet attainable

From the table tops
In the kitchen
To the rooftops
Of castles

We imagine
Create
No time to debate

Imagine
Visualise
Create

Create
Create

THOUGHTS

Sometimes
My thoughts
Are so fast
They lift me
Like a propeller

Levitating words
Into the clouds

I feel whole
Elevated
On a platform
Creating worlds

Scrambling
Receiving answers
Answers from God

I quickly pick up my pen
And try to work it all out

SPELL

And something changed
That day
The way she said
"If you say it three times
It's like a spell"

Like a mantra
Pulling worlds
Into existence

Worlds upon worlds
Created by words

The power
Of imagination

PROJECTOR HEART

I have hope in my heart
She shines
For me
Unwinds for me
Like a projector

INCEPTION

At the time
Of inception
Of any idea
I believe
We are
Not alone

When a soul arrives
When a star dies
When the idea
Of a song
Implants
And grows
Like wildflowers

We are not alone
Sweet child
We are not alone
We are not alone

You are not alone
You are not alone

I WONDER

I wonder if
One day

I'll find a space
Where I feel like
I fit in

Slot into place
Like a raindrop
That becomes
The ocean

OBSERVATION

There is a man
At the bottom of my drive
Maybe he is waiting for a ride

He noticed me watching
Black cloak and no hat
The rain pours over him

He pretends to look
At his watch

A social cue to show
He is sane
Not insane
For standing for ages
In the rain
In the middle of winter

No umbrella
Or raincoat
He stands

ARMY OF SPIDERS

I have an army of
Soldier spiders
In the shower room

Building cobwebs
On the ceiling
That I can't reach

Like universal
Comic book heroes
They climb so high

The perils
Of country life

THE CAT IN THE CUPBOARD

I think the cat's
In the cupboard
That's where he hides

He can see in the darkness
With his hypnotic eyes

The cat's in the cupboard
On all of my clothes
It's okay
As long as
He doesn't ruin them
I suppose

AND THEN THE RAIN CAME

And then the rain came
And poured upon
The trees
And fed the grass

The end of the heat wave
Washing everything clean
Creating mist on the horizon

And in the perfect skyline
I see you

Memories do not fade
But I consciously think now
And feel better

My system is healing
And my vortex
Is filled with hope

DANCING WITH CREATIVITY

It is fascinating
How creativity dances
And shape shifts
When we are
Left in solitude

In solitude
I am like liquid
I am molecules
I am earth
I am dust
I am blood
I am sweat
I am growth
I am hormones
I am earthling
I am bound
And unbound

All at once
With time
In this
Moment

SILLY CAT

I left the window
Open for you
Silly cat

And the wind
Rolls and roars

And old souls
Move in and out
And I capture
A thought

I write it down
With a purple pen

Bending the rules
It's easy

Thoughts and stories
Spill through me

On this fresh
Sunday morning

FOUR WALLS

When I rest
Allow boredom
Or, let's say,
Space to kick in

Well, that's when
There is room
Room to write

Between these
Four walls

In this dimension
Something ignites
Inside

Inside this head
This heart
This gut biome

This chaotic blend of
Acid and alkaline soup
Sending messages

I get up and brush
My teeth

And hope there is not too much
Fluoride in this paste
That I lace
Across my toothbrush

Mirror talks to me
Shows me my frizzy hair
She's been busy

In electric dreams
By night
Seven hours sleep

Frizz shows up
To say
Hey girl
It's a new day, girl

I say
I love you
Planting seeds

I love you
I love you
I love you

NEIGHBOUR'S CAT

Sliding
Gliding
Down the Velux window
On a rainy day

The neighbour's cat
Comes over the roof
To play

The timing ain't right
He's out of sight
I hear his paws
As he slides

Slides
Glides

I unroll the blinds wide
Daylight shines through
And the dotted
Eccentric cat
Meows louder
Than before

Meows some more
Echoing through
The village

I open the window
And he jumps on in

Dirty paws on carpet
He makes an awful racket

Meows and meows
Asking for a packet
A packet of meat
He knows I have in
Just for him

The neighbour's cat
He is not mine
But he seems to take up
A lot of my time

THE UNIVERSE IN YOUR TEACUP

Welcome worlds
Worlds of kindness
Gratitude and hope

Dance with
The universe
In your teacup

Read tea leaves
Like *Reader's Digest*

Cook with love
Make love with love
In tune
With my guitar
Strings

And the frequency
Of my favourite
Plant

Today is a good day
A good day
To stand tall

SECTION 2

—

NATURE AND HEALING

I FOUND YOU IN A RAINBOW

I found you
In a rainbow

In a moment
I felt lost

I found you
In a rainbow

When something
Good happened

I found you
In a rainbow

When I needed
A sign

Answers to a question
Responded using elements

Answers communicated
Between worlds

ARE YOU THERE?

Are the fields cluttered
With spirits?

Is that what the wind is?
All the lost loved ones?
Do I find you in the wind?

As you brush through my hair
Are you here?
Everywhere

Employed by the atmosphere
To shift us all
Into the next day?

MOTHER EARTH (RED BENCH)

And I sit on this red wooden bench
Listening to serene high-pitched tones
A meditation track for walking

The hills have a mist over them
The music is otherworldly
And I have this feeling
Am I ready to go?

To rise over these green fields
With the mist?
And become part of the universe?

Am I done here?
Or is there more to live for?

As my tired eyes blink
Into the distance
The sun comes out
The warmth hits my face
And I feel that is my answer

Comforted by Mother Nature
She soothes me
With yellow heat

The scent of earth
Fills me up
With afterglow

Afterthought

A thought
I still have more life to live
My life cycle is still
To be reckoned with
I am a beacon of hope

Resilience kicks in
Inherited from my grandmother
And my mind survives

A lingering thought that soon left
As the sun hit my face
And I listened to the universe
For she loves me
My Mother Earth

PETALS

Fractal patterns
From God

Geometrical states
Geometric shapes
Collide
And photosynthesize

They are truly alive
Those petals

OVERGROWN GARDENS

Bees can build
In overgrown gardens

Their nectar
Is their life

For every overgrown garden
Beauty is born

COCOON (CFS)

I cradled myself
Made my own cocoon
My own womb
All by myself
In my own room

Healing
Feeling
Breathing you in
And out

The universe
She heals me
Deep from within

I fly through time
And I wait
Until the moment

I feel fine again

SNOWFLAKES

You bring me snowflakes
In winter
You serve them up cold
I didn't ask you to

Memories of the sound
Of lawnmowers
On hot summer days

Your gaze
Upon mine
Like sunshine

The smell of you
Intoxicating
Addictive
Adorable

Sinking into my soul
You serve me hope
In your hands
And it lands differently
To what I expected

Life path hits a crossroad
And I am a startled rabbit

Hoovering out the habits
Of a lifetime

So I can learn to love again
Like I did back then

When you handed me
Those snowflakes
Of imagination

All those years ago

BLUE SKIES

Accidental magic
Comes from the tragic
Days gone by

The love, the loss
All bleed into you
And out towards the sky

Bleed it out
Into the trees
And the green

And they cry for you
With you

The birds fly
And carry this burden
So you don't have to

SUPERCONSCIOUS MIND

Superconscious mind
Awareness in my flow
Walking through space
From one day to the next

Moon upon moon
Sun upon sun
Glow down on me

Refreshing, renewing
Bleeding energy
Over and over

We grow
We sing
We reap what we sow

Planting seeds
For the children
Of tomorrow
Love them
With eyes of kindness
They will shine

MATRIX OF MAGPIES

A matrix of magpies
Fly past the window
Six for gold

I am sold
On the idea
I am due a windfall

Like an optimistic
Alchemist
I smile

I am an optimist
About all of this
Thank you

THE THUNDERSTORM

The thunderstorm
It woke me
Provoked me to think

All at the brink of dawn
I lost track of time
In and out of dream state

Waiting for you
Ideas flowing
In the dark of night
The seeds of thought
Open doors

Channelling channels
Of my mind

I eventually find my R.E.M

DOTS UPON DOTS

Dots upon dots
Lines in the road
Unfolding matters
That don't really matter
They are not the answers

You were sent to unearth more
Look deeper

OBSERVER

I observe my thoughts
I am the observer
I control how fast
They move
I can quiet them down

I can be peaceful
And breathe deeply
Into the heart
Intermittent silence

I create much needed
Interludes
As I find calm
The body is relaxed

CLEANSE ME

Early morning light
Thank you
Cleanse me

Lend me your
Unidentifiable hands
And walk me through the day
With the heat of the sun
That shines discreetly
Through a window

But who feels it?
Who sees it?

The blessed
Wake up child

This is a new day

REFLECT

When the daylight
Shatters the mirror
That has seen
Many rooms

As the dawn breaks through
Do you stand and contemplate
The forgotten tomorrows

It will not seek
No longer see?

OCEAN STILL

I have a quiet mind today
Can't see as many words
The ocean is still

Tranquil
I'm not used to this
I pick up my pen
And I'm writing
In a gentle slow manner
Feels different

I must get back
To meditation
And catch my flow
Create flow

A little bit of chaos
Fast moving stream
I can't stand still
I like to keep moving

Dreaming of running
Dreaming of walking
For miles

Lost in and out
Of cobbled streets
Running in and out
Of houses

I wake up from a vivid dream
And the ocean is still

BLUEBELLS (SONG LYRICS)

Bluebells
And blankets made of gold
Secrets stolen
Never to be told

Dangers
That prevent us
From getting old
Lullabies
That set us up for life

A love that never dies
A love that makes you cry

April blue velvet
Beautiful skies

April blue velvet
Beautiful skies

THE MOON

The moon
She is seen
In one half
Tonight
But she is
Altogether
There

AUTUMN

Autumn is coming
Temperature
Drops

Born under
The autumnal
Equinox

Born when
Everything
Is ready
For regrowth
To renew

I remember
The cold
With fresh
Eyes

I dance
In my bedroom
To love songs

I renew
I renew
I renew

REVISIT

I'm going to revisit
This memory
Over and over
Until it feels like
Poetry

SECTION 3

—

LOSS AND LONGING

THE RAIN

Is it raining today
In your world?

As I sink
Into the thought
Of you
Going about
Your day

Does the rain
Hit your window
In the same way?

MOURNING

The morning
Loathes your cries
Systematic goodbyes
And showers of loss
Change the page
New age

Grateful for every moment-
No time is linear
We are here, all at once

ENVELOPE OF THE MIND

In an envelope
I put you
And sealed the folds

Put you way back there
Somewhere to hide

So that one day
When I unfold you
It's easy

FEAR

Do you wake up with THE FEAR sometimes?
I hate that

RELEASE

Release this pain body
A series of waves
Showing me my thoughts

Patterns
Diving me in
And out of time
I breathe
Exhale the pain

Sigh, fly
Breathe with me
Flow out
Gently breathing
Emotions in and out

And I glide through open skies
I breathe, I breathe, I heal

MEMORY COLLECTOR

Like a jumble sale
A sea of unwanted junk
Swimming through
Memories

Deck chairs
Carousels
The Eiffel Tower

Floating on waves
Rafters
Sorting compartments
Keep or delete

Some are worth
Keeping of course

FOREVER FRIEND

"I loved you so much
Until I just burst
Like a balloon"
You said

So poetic for a 16-year-old
Those words still
Resound in my head
Especially now you're dead

A card you once wrote

You're 16 and you're great
You're 16 and you're great
Don't get drunk
And act like a clown
'Cause you've got
The best arse in town

When I got pushed
Out of home
To my dad's

To live next door
But two or three houses
From you

You took me in
Like you were
My mother or father
Or even a brother

You helped fix my wounds
After leaving a violent home
And you didn't have a clue

You were grounded
A mum and dad and sister

You had a band
And all of your friends
And you welcomed me
Into your world

Friends forever
A proper bond

We even slit our arms
And rubbed bloods
To become
Blood brother and sister

That sinking feeling
Time stands still

Heart torn apart
My other half becomes zero
Because he too
Loved you so much

I think
I'm kinda
Okay now?

Is it you when
The light flickers?
Or when my computer
Turns on at night?

Was it you when my hair dryer
Turned on for no reason?

Was it you in every rainbow
When I was sad?

Was it you who put the pattern
On the steamed-up mirror
While I was in the shower
When no one else was around?

Either way
I find comfort in that
Those unexplainable moments
In life

Those connections between
Miracles and unimaginable moments
As we experience the tragic days
Gone by

It took 140 poems
To get to this
To pull you out
Am I fixed now?

NOON

It's quite easy to
Just jump back into bed
Isn't it?
The smell of heat
And fabric softener
Fills my air waves

And I dream of the ocean
Holding hands with you
As we navigate the sands

Crystal formations falling
As you pull grains
Into your palm
And let them go

Like you let them go
Like you let me go
Like you let them know

That everything is ephemeral
Everything is free
Navigate with this open spirit
As you look towards the sea
As it casts a new tide

And my thoughts
Ride on it
Cold and smooth
Fresh
And renewed

And I chose to dream of walking
These sands with you
With open arms

A strong heart
Filled with desire
For life
For you
For us

Sand grains
Fractal patterns of minute worlds
Remind us of the vast expansion
Of this multiverse

Glide with me
I see you

Look what you made me do
I wrote a poem for us

OPEN ARMS

If I danced
Under moonlight
Would you see me?

If I sang
In the sunlight
Would you hear me?

If I talked with rhymes
Would you listen?

If I reached out to touch you
Would you fall into my arms?

SYLVESTER'S TIME

The memory of
The euphoric anxiety

The day my cat died
Hit me again this morning

My heart beats faster
And reaches out
To that moment

Body sending endorphins
To cancel out the fear
I feel high

And in this moment
It's painful again

My lungs hurt
It's interesting
How grief
Affects the lungs

Sweet soul cat
We spent 23 years
Together

THE CHILL OF WINTER

I feel the chill of winter
As it reveals itself
In the darkness of the night
As I lie in bed
It hovers over my head

I feel the chill of winter
I observe my thoughts

They are ruminating
Creating panic
I try to force sleep

After being rudely awakened
By the creaking doors
I feel the winter
She is to return
And I am cold

ROAM

You can roam with me
You can roam with me
You can come home
With me

Take a dance with me
Take a dance with me

We could be happy
We could be happy

I can set you free

And you with me
We are fire

SOMEBODY'S SOMEONE

I decided I wanna be
Somebody's someone

This day
I see you
In me
Undercovers
As the lights go down

I wanna be
Somebody's someone

To have and to hold
We grow into each other
And share our full truth

TWO HEARTS

Two hearts
You cry in all
The same worlds
That I do

You hide behind
The same doors
As me

You open your heart
To others
As I do

Together
We should dance

MIDNIGHT WITH M.E/CFS

Air thick
Throat burn
2am wake up call

Body sleep
Please sleep
Into deep healing
Tranquil phase

I call upon you
To let me dream

THE JACKDAW

Jackdaw singing
In the midnight air
She knows despair
Like no other

When hungry
She plucks chicks
From their nest to eat
I've witnessed this

Every creature
Does what it must
To survive

Where there is dark
There is light
Where there is day
There is night

I have seen the dark
And I know the light
I own it in my heart
She glows for me
When hope is lost

And I look towards the sky
And cast out that jackdaw

DOORWAY

The thing is I'm locked
Into a doorway
Locked into a time
Locked into a fragment
Of your world

I wake up
Eat
What do I wanna wear today?
Do I need to wash my hair today?
What will I dream up today?

What's cooking in your garden?
I found you in every corner
Of my thought
A seed of joy

As I look upon the green hills
That go on for miles
Towards the motorway
I find delight in the
Crispy white frosty
Frozen peaks

Green and white
Illuminated
Under sunlight

Coated with lashings
Of fluffy cloud

I open my window
Breathe you in
Today is a good day

Cold air fills my lungs
And I am ready for you

No one said
It had to make sense

GLITCH

Just like my MacBook Pro
You were forced to sleep
But unlike my MacBook Pro
You had a human empire
In your heart

And memories
Stored for decades
And we can't turn
You back on
Or reboot you
And the IT department
Can't fix this

And it ain't just a glitch
This is real
And it hurts
And you cannot
Be replaced

OMNIPRESENT

Omnipresent
Effervescent
Dreamer

I see you
In every corner

Like a hoarder
I store you
In compartments

Sweep you under
A metaphorical carpet
And revisit
I renew

As I renew
I find you
In every corner

Forever present
Forever friend

MILES APART

When the sun is visually
So close to the moon
I find that pretty cool
So tangibly together
Yet so far apart

Almost equally symmetrical
Two circles of hope
One burning with fire
One cold and full of dust

Yet rotating and connected
Collecting our thoughts
As they look down on us

As I rest
And soak up the heat
As I dream of glory days
A warm chest
To rest upon
With my daydreamer head

I see this partnership
Moving and rotating
And orbiting around each other
For the love of the earth

But what if they
Just wanted to connect?
And touch hearts
Moon on sun
Sun on moon

It would destroy the land
And maybe each other
Trying to forget
The yearning to touch
As they cross paths
And spin in and out
Of each other's reach

For centuries upon centuries
They communicate in their own way

Gaze upon each other
Mirror each other
From this distance that
Keeps them together
Keeps everything together

When the clouds pass over
They whisper to each other
Cloud curtains of privacy

As they spin and dance
In the atmosphere
Free

Yet restricted
For their own safety
For our safety

They stick to their own axis
As they orbit Mother Earth

They dream of love
Over the Atlantic Ocean
And over Egyptian desert sands

As their focused
Geographical journey
Connects them
They shine
Each in their own way

Toward the light
Toward the night

Equally lit with love

Fact : The closest point that the moon can actually get to the sun is 146,692,378 km

HOPE YOU ARE SMILING NOW (SONG LYRICS)

Hope that you're smiling now
Hope that you're happy now
Hope that you're homeward bound
I can't picture you underground

I never lied to you
You never lied to me
I know I made you cry
You know you made me cry

I know you lost a friend
You know I lost a friend
I know it broke your heart

Heart on sleeve
Kicking up dirt
Kicking up dirt

Know, you got hurt
Know, you got hurt

Honestly

Heart on sleeve
Kicking up dirt
Kicking up dirt

You know I got hurt
You know I got hurt
Honestly
Kicking up
Kicking up dirt

Know, we got hurt
Know, we got hurt

Hope that you're smiling now
Hope that you are happy now

Tell me you're safe and sound
Can't picture you underground
Tell me you're safe tonight

TAPESTRY

Creating art
Makes me feel part
Of this life

-All of its tapestry-

I feel like the stitching
I feel like the seams

TIME IS NOT A GENTLEMAN (SONG LYRICS)

Time is not a gentleman
Moves fast when you're high
High
And slow when you're low

And time
The great healer
Oh where is
My destiny?

I'm gonna find the river man
But I guess I'll never know
Where he will be flowing
Where he will be going

Going
Gone

And all the flowers grow
And slowly fade
And all the flowers grow and dissipate

Time, time is not a gentle gentleman
Moves fast when you're high
And slow when you're low

I am gonna buy the moon
Upon a stick
And pretend that everything is mine

But still all the flowers grow
And slowly fade
All the flowers grow
And dissipate

And all the flowers grow
And slowly fade
And all the flowers grow
And dissipate
And time
Time is not a gentle gentleman

Moves fast when you're high
High
And slow

When you're low
When you're low
When you're low

A POSTCARD FROM BEYOND

I found you in a notebook
I thought that you were gone
I found you in a notebook
My favourite type of song
I found you in the midnight air

I found you in the tide
I saw you in the crescent moon
I could see how bright
You would shine

I found you in the letterbox
A postcard with a note
Spider-like hand-written
A message that you wrote

I put you in my notebook
In my notebook
I kept you there

As I open my notebook
I feel you everywhere

MORNING HAS SPOKEN

As I sit motionless
I hear the ocean
Ocean of your cries

How do I let you go?
How do I let you know?
I am afraid
To let go

To let live
To give myself a break
Jaw aches
Tension

Did I mention
I believe in angels?

I pick up a trail of thought
The ones and zeros
Equally divide

Devising ways to live
With ease
I parade into the day

THE RAIN AGAIN

I swear I can sense
The rain coming
I bring the washing in

It smells cold and smooth
The rain begins to pour
Tip taps on my shoulders
The first time
I've been touched
All day

I feel dark
I want the sunshine back
And the heaviness of my limbs
To leave

The clouds surround me today
I'm just waiting
For them to dissolve

Leaves fall to the ground
From the giant trees

Those fallen leaves
Lost like me

SECTION 4

—

CONNECTION AND TRANSFORMATION

MIRROR DANCE

When you mirror
You feel every version
Of you

A healing space
A place for resolve
A room to dance
Glancing in and out
Of rooms we left behind

In the eyes of our soul
As we mirror

We shatter thoughts
And become whole

TAKE IT EASY

Take it easy
On yourself

Car engines
Shift gear
Outside my window

The pace is slow here
In the countryside

Peaceful
As daylight
Lands
On windows
Not yet open

PINK PENS AND CANDY FLOSS

Pink pens
Parade
Across
This page

I am pink
Like bonbons
And candy floss

I am fairgrounds
I am love hearts

Pink pens
And good friends
Are sometimes
All a girl needs

DREAMING CHILD (SONG LYRICS)

Hope you lived all of your dreams
Hope you loved all that you've seen

Dreamer
Oh my dreaming child

Oh how good to be alive
Eyes open wild
Eyes open wide
Like a bird in the early morn

Dream, don't ever stop
Catching all that you've got
Hands full
Don't let them drop

Every dream
Every dream
Every dream

Do you know where the days go?
Do you know where the wind blows?

Only time

Let me read your mind

ANGELS AND SPIRIT GUIDES

Angels
And spirit guides
Meet me in other rooms
When I make peace
With the moment

I settle into the now
I settle into myself
I love myself
I am gentle
With my body

As I listen to angels
And spirit guides
I am protected
Protecting
My inner child

I am so gentle
Deepest mind
Centurion soul

In this mode
I withstand
The elements

MATRIX

I lost my matrix
Then I found it again

In a handful of beads
Beads of light

Coming towards me
Lighting my path

South to north rising
I found my matrix
In the palm of my hand

Unexpected
Yet delightfully delivered
In white light form

CHECKMATE

Positive people
Lift me up

Eyes on the goal
Riding on thoughts

Travelling light
Emotional state
In check

Checkmate
Today I win

SETTLING INTO MY OWN SKIN

The shallow depth
Of field is intriguing
And the *bokeh* lights
Blue faces
In the crowd
Blue
All sitting there
Staring at you

Capturing the performance
Your joy
Brings me joy

As you settle into your skin
You command the stage
Light reflects
On the audience's shoes

And the sound resounds
And moves through the amplifiers
And penetrates
My heart

Camera lens reflects and reacts
Focus smile
Eyes wide
We love you
They say

This moment in life
I capture
Your life

And I settle into mine
A little more
With a sense of achievement

WELL

I am well
I am well
I am well
I am well

I've never seen
A wishing well
In real life

I am a living
Well of hope

THE BUTTERCUP

She grew
From almost nothing
Alone surrounded by pebbles
A fraction of dirt

She created her own mound
Dancing in the sun
Yellow so bright

The wind blows
She sways
From left to right

Firmly standing tall
Shining so bold
For me
Striking yellow

TODAY

I am feeling strong today
Because last night
Before I went to sleep
I said I would
I said I should
So I am

Think about it?
Think about what you say
To yourself

Before you sleep
At night

Really
Do think about it

OPEN DOORS

Closer than before
She moves towards
The open door
And enters
A new chapter
She flies

GOALS

Bring your dreams
Down to earth
For a while
And know your worth
Solid in your goals
You will fly

I AM A WOMAN

I am a woman
I am grown
Aware of the thoughts
I own

Aware of all the
Beliefs I placed
Upon a pedestal
Unnecessary

I am a woman
I have grown
No longer
Afraid of
All the emotions
I have known

I am a girl
I am a child
I am the three-year-old
Running wild
In shopping centres

I am a dreamer
I own my thoughts

I am shifting
Through the
Ones and noughts

I am a child
Of the 80s and 90s

I am a child
Of the universe

I am effervescent
I am present
Here and now
Back then

I am a woman
Of this earth
I know my worth

I am
I am

I am here

HELLO WORLD

Hello world
I found you again
In warm
Peaceful evenings

Under the moonlight
Amongst the spiderwebs
Drinking tea

Inhaling the scent
Of earthly hay bales

I inhale
Exhale

Spin my world around
In seconds
Low to high
In moments

Connecting to the
DIVINE
In milliseconds

Reconnecting
Protected
By earth sounds
Earthbound
Moments

I am on top
On top of the world

In this moment
I think
I think
I blink into
Existence
With a warm
Smile

Lit by moonlight

HAPPY NEW YEAR

Happy New Year
Three cheers to progress
A handful of dreams
Desires, building
Wildfires in my heart

Keeping me warm
I am whole
In this wintery
Wonderland

As this year begins
I smell hope

NEW WAVES

There's something
Shifted
Lifted
Kind of drifted

It's a new day
A new way
To see life

Play with me
Laugh with me
Move with me
Through me

In this moment
Something shifted
Lifted me
Into someplace
New

And the pleasure
Is all mine
And I serve it
Back and forth
From my tongue
To yours

SUNFLOWER EYES

Blessed by the sun
With sunflower days
Her eyes wide open
She danced

STEP INTO MY FLOW

Step into a thousand
Tomorrows

What do you see?
Create those dreams
Create those dreams
With me

Step into my flow
Oh, tell me now, darling
Where would you like to go?

AFTERWORD

Stepping into my flow.
I feel this gave me the ability to heal. I feel something magic happens when you let the pen glide into the power of now and you get into this flow. This unique vortex, this universal connection. A collective consciousness.

On the following page is a poem I wrote at secondary school aged 17.

I wanted to leave a space for this version of my younger self here.

Thanks again for stepping into my flow.

WHERE DO ALL THE DAYS GO?

Where do all the days go?
Do they leave with the wind?

Leaving so fast you miss them
With a blink of an eye
It hurts

Where is tomorrow?
Is it all mine?
When will the bell
At the start of it
Begin to chime?

I reach out to touch it
Why won't it reach out for me?
Where will tomorrow be?

I search with my ears
I look with my eyes

Where do the days go?
Are they in my shoes?
No!

GLOSSARY

CFS/ME (Chronic Fatigue Syndrome/Myalgic Encephalomyelitis) is a condition that affects energy, movement and daily life.

MICHELLE HEIGHWAY is an award-winning filmmaker and photographer based in West Yorkshire, known for her critically acclaimed documentaries *Mr. Somebody?* and *Energy: A Documentary* about Damo Suzuki.

In 2024 Michelle Heighway was awarded funding from the Arts Council to develop her poetry practice. This is when Michelle Heighway was able to create her debut book *Step Into My Flow*.